Dad's Birthday Present

by Geoff Patton
illustrated by David Clarke

RISING★STARS

to the museum

to the school

Emily's house

to Sam's house

to Con's house

2

Lin's apartment

3

Hi. My name is Emily.
This is my family.

Dad

me
(Emily)

Molly,
my little sister

4

Puddle

Chapter 1
A Puddle in the House

We have a new puppy. Her name is
Puddle. We gave her to Dad for his
birthday. Dad said he *really* wanted
socks. He said that socks were *much*
easier to look after.

We said, 'Don't worry, Dad,
we will look after her.'

In the night Puddle cried. She cried
and cried and cried. But I didn't
hear her. I was wearing my new
woolly earmuffs. Molly didn't
hear her. She was sleeping under
the blankets.

Dad didn't hear her. He was
snoring too loudly.

But Ms Purtle, who lives next door, heard Puddle. Ms Purtle phoned Dad. Now Puddle sleeps with Dad. Molly says they look *so* cute.

We didn't know that Dad was *so* cuddly!

Chapter 2
A Walk in the Park?

When we go to the park, we say,
'Can we take Puddle?' Dad says
he *really* wants to take the car.
He says that the car is *much*
easier than walking Puddle.

We say, 'Don't worry, Dad,
we will look after her.'

On the way to the park Puddle pulls on her lead. She pulls and pulls and pulls. I say, 'Heel, Puddle,' and give her to Molly. Molly says, 'Heel, Puddle,' and gives her to Dad.

Dad says, 'Heel, Puddle,' but Puddle run away from him.

Puddle runs into Ms Purtle's garden.
Puddle really likes Ms Purtle's
garden. So *did* Ms Purtle.
We go to the park, while Dad
helps Ms Purtle in the garden.

We didn't know Dad *liked* gardening!

Chapter 3
In the Bath – Out of the Bath

When we are having a bath, we say,
'Can Puddle come in?' Dad says he
really doesn't think it's a good idea.
He says it is *much* easier to have a
bath without Puddle.

This is not a good idea.

We say, 'Don't worry, Dad,
we will look after her.'

In the bath Puddle shakes. She
shakes and shakes and shakes.
I say, 'Out, Puddle!' as the water
sprays. Molly says, 'Out, Puddle!'
as the water sprays.

Out, Puddle!

Dad says, 'Out, Puddle!' as the
water sprays.

Puddle runs out of the bathroom.
So does Dad. Puddle runs out of the
front door. So does Dad. Puddle runs
into the street. So does Dad. Puddle
runs into Ms Purtle. So does Dad.
We have a bath, while Dad takes
Ms Purtle to the doctor.

We didn't know that Dad
was *so* helpful!

Chapter 4
Sky High Puddle

When we are playing on the trampoline, we say, 'Can Puddle jump too?' Dad says he *really* doesn't think it's a good idea. He says it would be *much* easier to jump without Puddle.

We say, 'Don't worry, Dad, we will look after her.'

On the trampoline Puddle flies high.
She flies higher and higher and
higher. I say, 'Not too high, Puddle.'
Molly says, 'Not too high, Puddle.'

Dad says, 'Not too high, Puddle,'
but Puddle flies over the fence.

Puddle lands in Ms Purtle's yard.
Puddle runs into Ms Purtle's house.
Puddle really likes Ms Purtle's house.
So *did* Ms Purtle. We jump on the
trampoline, while Dad helps
Ms Purtle with the cleaning.

We didn't know Dad *liked* cleaning!

Chapter 5
Puddle the Watchdog

When our friends Jay and Fay call
to ask us over, we say, 'Can we take
Puddle?' My Dad says he *really*
doesn't think it is a good idea.
He says it would be *much* easier
for her to stay home.

We say, 'Don't worry, Dad,
we will look after her.'

But when Jay and Fay come to get us, Dad is asleep. He snores and snores and snores. We cover him with Molly's blanket.

We say, 'Don't worry, Dad, Puddle will look after you.'

Molly says, 'Puddle is the best birthday present Dad has ever had.' I think she is too. But maybe next year we will just buy him socks.

Survival Tips

1 Hide your shoes.

2 Hide your socks.

3 Hide all of your clothes.

4 Keep a spade handy. Puppies like to dig holes.

5 Keep paper handy. Puppies like to make puddles.

6 Ignore bad behaviour.

Riddles and Jokes

Emily	What did the dog say when he was jumped on by a tiger?
Ms Purtle	Nothing. Dogs can't talk.
Emily	Did you hear the one about the dog who ran 5 kilometres to get the stick? It was too far-fetched.
Molly	Did you hear about the dog who went to the flea circus? He stole the show!
Emily	Why did the dog howl?
Molly	Because it saw the tree bark.
Molly	What did the dog say when he sat on the sandpaper?
Emily	Ruff, ruff!